Seven Tales of Love

LINDA MAHKOVEC

Other Books by Linda Mahkovec

The Dreams of Youth

The Garden House

The Christmastime Series:

Christmastime 1940: A Love Story

Christmastime 1941: A Love Story

Christmastime 1942: A Love Story

Christmastime 1943: A Love Story

Contents

Juliet

Howard Ashbury strolled along Columbus Avenue, enjoying the fine weather – autumn in New York – a welcome break from the gray of Seattle. Something about the pulse of the city, the charm of the Upper West Side, brought back his younger self, and he felt happy, hopeful. He stopped in front of a little café, and, though it was too early for dinner, he decided to go in. He would read the new script over a glass of wine.

As he entered, he took in the exposed brick walls, the long windows, the candles just being lit in the softening light. Then his heart gave a little lurch when he saw her sitting there – Anna Avilov, his old Juliet. Suddenly, the twenty years since the production of *Romeo and Juliet* in San Francisco vanished.

My God, he thought. She's as beautiful as ever. There she sat, with a dreamy look in her eyes, pen poised in her hand as she searched for some word or phrase. She wore her hair loosely swept up, and the shimmering aquamarine blouse caught the color of her eyes. What was she searching for – some hidden world of beauty? What did she see?

Howard felt the old chivalrous urge to help her.

But Anna had never needed anyone. He remembered how they were all in love with her, in love with the beauty and charm she possessed. Men and women alike took to her, as did the audience. They all wanted some of whatever it was she exuded – to possess it, to be in its presence, however briefly. He remembered how she had felt pulled down by that hungry need from everyone, and had shied away from the very attention the other actors sought.

Perhaps feeling his gaze, Anna looked over at him. Their eyes met, and her brow furrowed as she tried to place him.

Howard gave a small, wry smile. Have I changed so much? he wondered.

He walked over to her. "Hello, *Juliet*," he said, hoping the name would bring back the memory of him. He waited a beat. "Don't you remember your old stage manager?"

Anna's eye widened as she gasped. "Howard!" She jumped up and hugged him. "I can't believe it! Oh, how wonderful! Can you sit with me? I just can't believe it!" In between each exclamation she searched his face, stepping back a bit to take in the changes.

He had forgotten how petite she was. She had to stand on her toes to kiss his cheek.

Howard pulled out the chair across from her, and waited for her to take her seat. He then sat down.

They ordered a bottle of wine. As Howard crossed his legs and turned the saltshaker around in his fingers, Anna clapped her hands in delight.

"Oh! You still wear red socks. You haven't changed. Not a bit. Still so handsome and dapper!"

Howard smiled, realizing that it was ridiculous for her words to mean so much to him. But his recent failed affair had left him wounded and unsure of himself.

They talked and laughed and caught up on the last twenty years. Howard told her that he was still working as a stage manager, the last twelve years in Seattle. He described some of the more memorable productions.

Anna filled him in on the rather haphazard path she had taken. When she moved to New York eighteen years ago, she had found work as an off-off-Broadway actress, filling in the gaps between shows with waitressing and temping. The years since had been marked by a variety of unrelated jobs, a bit of travel, and, ten years ago, the meeting of her husband.

Howard was disappointed to hear that she had given up acting after she married. But Anna said it was writing that she had always felt more at home with.

"Yes, I remember that. You were always writing during rehearsals. What was it you used to say? That you were trying to create the world you were forever in search of. Have you found it? Or have you created it?"

Anna laughed. "Neither, I'm afraid. It still eludes me."

"And are you still interested in theater?"

"Yes, of course." She glanced at her watch. "As a matter of fact, my husband has tickets for tonight. Dinner, and then Chekhov. He's picking me up here. I'm so happy you'll be able to meet him."

She went on to say that she had written some one-act plays and was working on a screenplay. As he listened, he observed the old air of wistfulness about her.

After two hours of talking, Howard noticed that evening had crept closer to their window. The candles on the tables and the lights outside shone brighter now, against the dark. That artful thrill of early evening filled the air, and shone from the faces of the couples filling the tables next to them, and from people hurrying by outside – the thrill that the night might hold something wonderful.

Howard knew that her husband would be there soon to take her to dinner, yet there was so much more he wanted to know. He gave a small ironic smile; she still had the power to stir up a hunger in her audience. He poured the last of the wine into their glasses, and asked if she remembered William Chase.

"Of course, I do! Benvolio. Or was it Balthasar? You'd think I'd remember." She looked above his head, scanning the stage of so long ago, squinting ever so slightly, as if the stage lights were still in her eyes.

Howard also wondered how she could forget. "Benvolio," he said. "And so terribly in love with you."

Anna nodded. "Benvolio. Of course." She took a sip of wine. "What ever became of him? Do you know?"

"Yes, as a matter of fact, I ran into him last year in Portland. He became a lawyer, of all things."

"A lawyer?" Anna asked, surprised. "Good for him."

Howard had always wondered if Anna was aware of the effect she had on people. He thought it unfair that beauty could so effortlessly cause pain to others. He recognized his buried resentment, mixed with admiration, for all the things she represented to him. He had never wanted to sweep her into his arms, or make love to her. Rather, he had wanted to *be* like her, to move through the world with such power and beauty and ease.

Howard would later blame the wine for making him press on as he did. His words came out almost accusingly. "William told me that he never really got over you."

Anna leaned slightly back, as if in defense. Her full lips shaped her words as she spoke.

"Well, there was never anything between us. I certainly never encouraged him. I guessed he had feelings for me, but you know how that is – how often that happens in an emotionally charged cast."

Howard nodded and looked down. The image of the beautiful Roberto filled his mind: how their eyes had met across the stage, how their love had developed, those first perfect months. With bitterness, he remembered the torch he had carried for Roberto, long years after being rejected.

"You know," said Howard, allowing some of his resentment to creep into his tone, "William always thought it was because of his height. He thought you never took him seriously."

This was actually Howard's belief, but he assumed this must be the case since William had been strikingly handsome. "That was one of the reasons he went into law, he said. More weight – or height, in his case."

Howard waited for her answer. He wanted to know whether he had been correct all these years in attributing to Anna a certain small-mindedness; or whether he had ungenerously projected onto her the reasons for his own unrequited loves.

Again, Anna squinted into the past. "Yes. I remember him saying something about that once. He invited me to dinner, but I just wasn't interested. He asked if it was because of his height. I think I laughed out loud at such a ridiculous notion. I didn't have the heart to tell him it was his whininess that made him unattractive. It was so off-putting. Do you remember? He complained about everything and everyone."

Anna swirled the wine around in her glass, and smiled. "Besides, I've always preferred short men. A better fit, you know."

Howard snapped upright in surprise – both by her candor, and by his mistaken assumption. He had always believed that height was one of those universally desired attributes – attributes that he, for the most part, did not possess.

He responded with a simple, "Oh?" and began turning the saltshaker around again. His thoughts tripped over themselves as he attempted to reorganize them, realizing that he had indeed misjudged Anna – and perhaps his own beloved – all these years.

Anna spoke as if merely stating a fact, but a sly seductiveness played about her lips.

"Yes, whether kissing when standing, or cuddling at night, or..." Her aquamarine blouse shimmered in the candlelight as she gave a light shrug.

Howard quickly replayed the arguments with Roberto. He had always assumed that Roberto had rejected him because of his age, ethnicity, or some other quality over which he had no control. For the first time, the thought gripped him: What if Roberto had simply found him boring? Or, God forbid, whiny?

Then, as if on cue and choreographed to maximize the insight into his own failed affairs, in walked Anna's husband – short, if not shorter, than William Chase. He was equally as handsome, though, Howard had to admit, in a more genial manner.

Anna's whole being surged with pleasure at the sight of her husband's flashing smile and warm eyes. She stood to embrace him – in a comfortable fit, Howard noticed – and introduced them.

As she slipped on her wrap, the three of them spoke briefly and exchanged business cards. Howard declined the invitation to join them for dinner, but promised to stay in touch.

Anna and her husband waved good-bye and left the café.

Howard sat back down at the table and tried to put his ruffled thoughts back in order, tapping the saltshaker up and down. As he shook his head at life's vanities and wretched misunderstandings, the beautiful Anna Avilov tapped on the window and blew him a kiss, her arm linked with that of her Romeo.

Offering

After years of saving and planning, Ellie had finally moved to the big city. One of the waiters she worked with told her about the weekend flea market, and she decided to visit on her next Sunday off.

She had picked up every available double shift and now had a whole day to herself. She dressed in a long, blue, beaded skirt and a gauzy white top. It was almost with a sense of wonder that she assessed her reflection in the mirror – she was now a part of this city of dreams!

The market vibrated with color and sound. A slight breeze blew against her skin as she wandered from one stall to another. There were so many different types of people and objects. Like a huge, exotic bazaar. She smiled when a small child riding on her father's shoulders waved, trailing rainbow ribbons behind her.

The scents of sandalwood and musk drew her to a table full of Egyptian oils and wares. She leaned over to admire the exquisite perfume bottles delicately painted in thin gold and rose and blue. The heady aromas and the beauty of the vials stirred something deep inside her; images of desert market towns and strange-sounding words came to her mind. She would return to this stall.

"That's my personal favorite," said the vendor of pretty floral and embroidered scarves. The gray-haired man sat shirtless in a lawn chair, as if he were sunning himself on vacation.

Ellie laughed to see that around his neck was the same scarf that she held in her fingers. He wore his loose against his wrinkled, tanned chest and belly.

"Go ahead," he said. "Try it on."

"Oh, I'll be back. I only just got here," Ellie said, as she wandered to the next booth. She wanted to see everything the market had to offer before she decided on her purchases – buying only what she loved most.

She stopped to admire some painted Russian dolls, laughing as she got tangled in the fluttering skirts hanging in the neighboring stall.

All the world is in this bazaar, she said to herself. She passed a table of African carvings and woven baskets, another of antiques and old photographs.

Here was a children's clothing booth. She gazed up at a little girl's dress flapping in the breeze. So sweetly blue and soft. As she reached up to touch the gauzy fabric, the woman behind the table asked, "For your baby?"

"Oh, no – I was thinking of my niece. But she's almost six now."

"Oh, she too big. This for baby."

"Yes." Ellie suddenly felt foolish.

But here was a display of brightly colored toys and dolls. She would find something for her niece at this table. Yes, she would come back and look at the dolls.

The breeze carried the high and low notes of wind chimes – clear, penetrating, ringing through the mixed sounds of laughter, bartering, shouts. Then, across the way, glittering in the sun, she saw strands and strands of beaded necklaces, draped languidly over old mirrors.

She crossed over and lifted a few strands in her palm. "Are these old?" she asked, immediately enchanted with them.

"Some of them," answered the woman at the stall. "Most are strung with old beads, 1920s style. Try one on." The vendor wore several strands together. A floppy straw hat shaded her face, but she was still sunburned.

These were expensive compared to the other things Ellie had seen. A pregnant woman and her friend stopped and began to try on different combinations, laughing as they encouraged each other in their choices.

As Ellie sorted through the long necklaces, visions of beaded flapper dresses and sumptuous soirees filled her mind. She decided she would definitely come back to this stand, and buy the beautiful midnight-blue and gold strand. It would be a symbol of all the dreams to come.

There was a table of orchids and bonsai, another of burning incense and candles, others of vintage clothing. In her labyrinthine wandering, she inadvertently passed the table of beads again. The pregnant woman and her friend were deciding among several strands. Then she noticed that the blue and gold necklace she had so admired was already gone. That was fast, she thought, trying not to be disappointed. Oh well, there were others equally beautiful.

Ellie was just about to retrace her steps to her favorite stalls and carefully make her purchases when two girls of about ten years old ran up to her.

Handing her a bag, one of them said, "That man said you dropped this, and to give it to you." They giggled and ran off.

"What man? This isn't mine."

She opened the bag, hoping for a clue to return it to its owner.

A sweaty dread filled her when she saw its contents. Inside were all the things she had desired, fondled, admired – attached her dreams to. Jumbled together were the little blue dress and Egyptian vials, the strand of beads and the scarf, the Russian doll she hadn't even wanted.

Ellie stood frozen, her eyes scanning the seething crowd. In all that blur of humanity, only one figure remained still. Her lips parted in horror, her nostrils flared in anger. What would have been genuine pity for him, instead turned into slow-mounting revulsion – for so involving her. Had he been in an accident? Had he been born that way? Her mind reeled and stumbled as her thoughts sought escape. She looked down at the gauzy blue dress in her hand, and then back at the man.

With a crooked gesture, he moved his head, for her to accept his offering.

Ellie was afraid of the look of pain on his face, the rising nausea in her stomach. She set the bag down on the ground, slowly shaking her head no, no, no.

With a sense of shame, she turned and pushed her way through the gaudy, pressing crowd. Leaving behind her the bag of pretty dreams.

Peonies

Eva opened the door to a huge bouquet of flowers filling the doorway and almost blocking the giver.

"Oh, you brought me peonies!" she cried, kissing her boyfriend.

She gave a quick glance at his hair. She always felt slightly hostile towards him when he got his hair cut so severely. She buried her face in the mix of pale pink and magenta flowers, and inhaled their scent as she carried them into the kitchen.

"These are one of my favorite flowers. Thank you!" She filled a vase with water and began to trim the stems.

He followed her into the kitchen. "I thought they were your favorite."

"They are, among others." She noticed the look of disappointment on his face, and his very short hair. "But that's all right. I mean, I love these."

"I know it's all right."

He loosened his tie and went to the refrigerator for the beer that she always kept for him. "Besides," he said, kicking the door shut, "you can only have one favorite flower."

"I guess I can have as many as I want." She began to list them as she arranged the peonies in the vase. "Lilacs and wisteria, lily-of-the-valley, violets." She placed the vase in the center of the table. "And roses, of course – the garden kind." She watched him lean against the table and take a long swig from the bottle.

"Busy day?" She walked up to him and stroked his back.

He nodded, and appeared fatigued.

She kissed his cheek. "I'll just be a minute."

Eva went into her bedroom to change, continuing her list to herself as she undressed.

"Chrysanthemums in the fall, heather, and there's nothing like daffodils in the spring – except tulips. And hyacinths."

"I hope you don't mind an early dinner," he called out.

"No, that's fine!" she answered, slipping a long pink and black print dress over her head.

Eva watched him through her bedroom doorway as she dressed. He always seemed uncomfortable in her apartment, stiff and hard-edged. He never knew what to make of the dried roses and old postcards, her seashells and ribbons. She observed him as he stared at the pile of pinecones and leaves that she had gathered from her walk in the park. He picked up a pine cone and held it loosely. Then with a slight shake of his head, he set it back down.

She dabbed perfume on her wrists and neck. She had been so happy before he arrived. What happened? She loved peonies. She followed his reflection in her mirror. He appeared disoriented, as if he didn't know what to look at and what to touch. He sat on the couch and turned on the television.

"How does Italian sound?" he asked over the sound of the TV. "You know, the place on Ninth?"

"I love that place!" She thought her voice sounded overly cheerful.

She wrapped a scarf around her neck, and looked at herself indifferently in the mirror. Then she walked to the bedroom window and parted the curtains. She gazed out at the trees, the cloudy sky, remembering. Something about that kind of sky and breeze.

He called out from the living room. "Ready?"

*

After dinner, they strolled for a while, looking at the different shops. Down the street, the sunset sky framed the silhouette of the old church. The view of it always filled Eva with images of medieval cities, walled gardens, cobblestoned streets. "I love that old tower."

"What tower?" he asked, puzzled. "You mean the steeple?"

She nodded, and let her gaze follow the tower up to the darkening sky.

He stopped as they passed a flower stall. "Do you want anything?"

She gave him a quick glance. Had he already forgotten the peonies? He suddenly seemed to remember, and looked away.

They approached her brownstone, knowing that he wouldn't come upstairs.

"I have an early flight in the morning." He held her tenderly and sighed. "I'll call you when I get back."

She nodded.

They kissed, and parted.

*

Eva took off her shoes, and walked into the kitchen without turning on the light. Outside the window, the leaves of the tree moved slowly, almost languidly, as if under water.

She sat at the table and beheld the vase of peonies. They had meant so much to her, at some point in her life. She conjured up the peonies of her childhood – huge bushes in the crook of the old hedge. Odd-shaped anthills of cones and valleys all around the bushes. "This is what the moon looks like," she had told her younger brothers. Another memory of playing fairies with her sisters, ducking and hiding behind the bushes at twilight.

She lifted one peony and pressed its velvety petals across her face. She plucked a petal and let it drop to the floor. Then another and another, saying, "He loves me, he loves me not. I love him, I love him not."

With the second flower she added, "He never could have loved me. I never would have loved him."

But this was taking too long. She pulled several petals out at a time until all that remained in the vase were stems and leaves. She tilted her head at the pile of pink petals on the floor, and nodded.

"It looks good this way."

Eva sat in the half-light, the underwater world outside filling the kitchen with its soft shadows. She tried to remember those other peonies – how the white ones seemed to glow at dusk. Globes of soft white among dark green leaves. Still and distant.

The Asking

It had been more than twenty years since she had danced. Dancing wasn't a part of her husband's character, along with many other things she used to delight in. In the early days, they had moved to music in her apartment. He had tried, for her sake. And yet, in him she had the security that she had never found with anyone else. Before him, there were always the betrayals, small or large, that spoiled her relationships and made her unsure of people. Her marriage was not what she had dreamed of in her youth – but then, neither were the betrayals. At least he was true, devoted, loyal. Rock solid. It had been easy to give up the superficial accessories of love.

So what was this desperate stirring inside her now? This night as she danced to the rhythms of the music, with the man whose hand gently held hers, moving together as if in long familiar ease? Delight, excitement, the thrill of the dance, as in her youth. That dream was supposed to be long dead, long ago replaced with more reassuring, dependable matters. What was it doing so achingly awake in her now – in all of its glittering, hopeful youthfulness?

An alarm shot through her. This feeling did not belong to her, the fiercely loyal woman of unshakable convictions. It was because of the music, surely, the warm breeze, the Old World balconies, the tiny soft lights in the night.

It wasn't the kindness in his eyes, the flashes of laughter, the protective arm around her shoulder, the earthy connection to the rhythms of life.

No, it was the soft crashing of the waves, the shimmering pink and melon sunset. It was the sly promise that night weaves into its beginning. It was all that – and he was just a part of it, surely.

Unexpectedly, life was offering her a choice. All she had to do was embrace it. The choice was there, offered to her with simple outstretched hands – no demands, nothing but the sweetness of human warmth. The choice to connect with life one more time before age and plodding routine took over for good.

Or, to stay true to her old self, to the woman she thought she was.

This sudden feeling was not part of her code of living. Such a breaking of that code would leave her unsure of anything ever again.

Or, would it open her up to a whole new way of being – once more connected, once more happy and hopeful, her old buried self awake again, bursting into blossom after long dormant years?

Would it be sadder to give in? Or sadder to deny?

Either way was crushing. The question kept rolling in the surf of her mind, along with the feeling that she had recaptured her beauty, her liveliness, the agility and freedom of movement that she thought she had lost.

Then, slowly, there in her mind, was her husband's face, there with his gaze – the eyes that always asked, that always expressed love and desire for her. Her heart was pierced with tenderness for him, for all their faults and failures over the years. They were bound, bound – no matter what dreams of beauty might cross her path.

Her excuse was sore feet and age when she declined to dance further, when she took her seat, and watched the other dancers dance under the tiny lights.

Romantic Love

Laura was the first to arrive at the restaurant. She took a booth in the corner, where she could watch for her friend, a fellow English professor she had known for years. She smiled when a few moments later Deborah make her entrance – brisk, a big wave, close-cropped hair, red lipstick.

Deborah gave her a hug and made kissing sounds. "So good to see you! You look fabulous!"

They settled in, ordered their meals and glasses of wine, and picked up where they last left off.

Laura observed her old friend make the usual adjustments to her clothing: collar pulled up, sleeves tugged down, jacket pulled together, shawl adjusted artfully over her shoulders. And then to the things on the table: flowers and candle rearranged, bread plate moved aside to make room for her folded arms.

"How are your classes?" Laura asked.

"Great! Everything's great! Did I tell you that Lucinda's pregnant?"

"Every time I see you," smiled Laura.

Deborah laughed. "I'm so excited. I'm going to be a grandmother. Imagine that. Me! I'm going to Boston over the break to help her shop for baby furniture. She and Kamal are fixing up the second bedroom as the nursery. Though if I know Luci, she'll keep the baby in her room.

"Just like you did. It's wonderful you two are so close."

Deborah's eyes filled with pride. "She's my life. I only wish she lived closer."

"Do you think Russ will play much of a role as grandfather?"

Deborah snorted at the preposterous idea. "Not if he stays true to his selfish self and wife number three. Did I tell you she's thirty? Almost the same age as Luci! I'm *so* disgusted with him."

"Well, at least you produced an incredible child together."

"Yes, we did." Deborah clinked her glass to Laura's. "How are you? How's Peter?"

"Fine. He's away for two weeks. It's crazy how much I miss him when he's gone. At first, I kind of enjoy it. I get so much done. Then after a while, I start counting the days until he returns. But I'm making progress on my paper, and am keeping up with my classes."

Deborah grabbed Laura's wrist for emphasis as she said, wide-eyed, "I had such a row in class today! Who would have thought that this younger generation could be so attached to outdated concepts?"

"Oh, they can be as traditional as any other generation," Laura laughed. "What concept are they holding on to?"

Deborah pursed her mouth in disbelief. "Romantic love! I did my best to explain that it's nothing more than a social construct to keep repressive practices intact. A biological ruse, lust sublimated to keep the species going. But the majority of class tried to refute this, citing literature." Deborah waved her hand in the air. "*Romeo and Juliet*!"

Laura felt a little stab. "Well, that's just a theory, after all. *You* may not believe in romantic love but that doesn't mean it doesn't exist."

"Oh, come on! Don't tell me *you* believe in it?"

"What about me and Peter? We've been together for twenty-six years, are too old to have children, but we're still passionate and in love. It's about something far more profound and lasting than lust." She cut Deborah off as she tried to interrupt. "And *Romeo and Juliet* is hardly about procreation, but about something essential to the human condition."

Deborah nodded and took a sip of wine. "Yes. Hormones."

Her dismissive response spurred Laura to counterattack. "Then, according to your theory, there is also no such thing as filial or parental love. That, too, is just a biological ruse to keep the species going."

Deborah now felt the stab. "That's completely different!"

Laura laughed. "Well, as usual, we agree to disagree."

The waiter made a timely appearance with their salads. As he offered pepper, Deborah's cell phone rang. She glanced at the number. "It's Luci — do you mind?"

Laura motioned for her to take the call. She couldn't help thinking what a hard-nosed theorist Deborah had always been. She smiled as she imagined Deborah's response: "And you're a sentimental Victorianist!"

Laura gazed out the window. A man carrying a bunch of flowers hurried by. An older couple strolled by arm in arm. At the table across from her, a man and woman linked hands. Laura let her mind wander. *Even if it is a social construct, it's one of the better ones we've come up with. Lust?*

A ruse? Passion? Romance? What does it matter what name we give love? Love by any other name…

The conversation turned to books, health, and the pros and cons of going gray. As the meal progressed, visions gathered in the backs of their minds.

In one, Lucinda's delight at the chic, black maternity smock, and stopping for lunch while they shopped for baby furniture.

In the other, the countdown. Three more days – and then the embrace, the conversations and walks, reaching out to feel his warm skin in the middle of the night.

Caramelized Onions

Olivia held the phone and stared out at the falling snow. She was silent as Suzanna casually mentioned that she was going to bring a friend along to dinner that night – Mark, her husband's old college friend, who was in town for a few days.

"Just to make it an even six."

Olivia resented the intrusion. "You know I hate to be set up."

"It's not a set up. But you might like him. He's very nice. And good-looking."

"It was supposed to be just you and Janet and your husbands. I hate cooking for strangers."

"I'm sorry, it was an impulse. He's here on business and I thought, he's single, you're single…"

"Because I want to be."

"Come on, Olivia. It's been over five years. It's time you —"

"See you at seven." She hung up.

Olivia picked up the framed photograph on the desk. A handsome man laughed into the camera, shielding his eyes from the sun. She was used to speaking out loud to him. She lived alone and didn't have to worry about what anyone thought.

"How can they know that I still feel you here? That after I first saw you, it was too late for anyone else. With all our faults, all our long years of trying, I would not have traded it for anything."

She kissed the photograph and put it back on the desk. The snow lightly piled up on the window ledge.

*

Later in the day, Olivia set the table, and carefully arranged the flowers she had bought earlier. Some branches with bright red berries had caught her eye at the florist's down the street. She now mixed them with white tulips and pine boughs — perfect for the season.

It was just yesterday that he had brought her flowers. Yesterday, thirty years ago. She loved the way flowers mattered to him, how he took his choices seriously, trying to please her with something new. She smiled as she remembered how he once brought her a bouquet of beautiful mixed roses, and shook his head.

"No," he said. "I'm not satisfied. There's no fragrance."

And the birthday he couldn't be there. When she arrived home, she followed a trail of pink and red roses that led to the bedroom. On their bed, spelled in petals, *Happy Birthday, My Love*. She left them on the bed that night. She still had a few of them in her jewelry box. Dry, brown petals now.

Olivia looked at the long skirt and emerald blouse that she had earlier laid out on her bed. She put them back in the closet, and decided on a black turtleneck sweater and black pants. She was looking forward to seeing her friends. And they wouldn't stay long.

*

Olivia answered the doorbell, relieved that Janet and her husband were the first to arrive. By the time Suzanna, her husband, and his friend, Mark, arrived, Olivia was in good spirits and was enjoying the evening.

Over wine and hors d'oeuvres, they swapped travel stories, caught up, and laughed. After a while, Olivia left to prepare the meal. Suzanna followed her into the kitchen.

"Well, wasn't I right? Isn't he charming and funny? And handsome?"

Olivia set out the vegetables for the pasta and began to rinse them.

"Yes. He is."

"I'd say you had a lot in common. It looked like you two had a real conversation going there. What were you talking about?"

"Our spouses. How wonderful they were. How many years we were married."

"Oh, for God's sake." Suzanna opened another bottle of wine. "Looks like I'm going to need this." She started to leave, then turned to Olivia. "What if he wants to see you tomorrow? Would you say yes?"

Olivia patted the vegetables dry and set them next to the cutting board. "No. He's very nice, but please don't encourage him."

Suzanna shook her head and left the kitchen.

A few minutes later, Mark came in and asked if there was anything he could help with. They talked and laughed a bit, then Olivia handed him the salad and asked him to fill the glasses on the table. She would be out soon. He placed his hand on her shoulder before he left, and smiled.

Olivia took her time chopping the onions for the sauce. She could hear laughter coming from the living room, and was glad they were having a good time. They really were a great bunch of people. Yes, she was lucky in her friends.

*

Olivia didn't know how long she had been staring into the pan when she realized that tears were dropping into the burning onions. She removed the pan from the burner and turned off the stove.

She looked down at the onions. I could call them caramelized, she thought. With my old love, I would do just that. We would laugh, and I would simply continue adding tomatoes, capers, olives, herbs. And it would taste like the pasta dish from that restaurant we used to go to, the one with the red walls. We would light the candles, and you would say how good it was. I would see your face in the soft light, and I would have to stop and reach out to stroke the curve of your cheek, and again admire the beauty of your eyes.

Olivia turned away from the stove and sat down. The voices and memories and smell of burnt onions began to mix and blur.

Recipe for Caramelized Onions

Chop one large onion.
Add two tablespoons olive oil, and a dash of salty tears.
Mix in the sweetness of memory, and stir.
In the time your mind wanders, the onions will begin to turn.
Lift the lid – and behold! Caramelized onions.

Solomon Grundy

Solomon Grundy,
Born on Monday,
Christened on Tuesday,
Married on Wednesday,
Took ill on Thursday,
Grew worse on Friday,
Died on Saturday,
Buried on Sunday.
And that was the end
Of Solomon Grundy

If that isn't the dangdest thing. Here I am, ninety-five years old, and something new has happened to me. Just when I was sure that there was nothing left for me to experience, along came Life and tapped me on the shoulder saying,

Hey there, Sol – look around. There's still a thing or two I want to show you.

I'll grant you, it's nothing earth-shattering, and yet, here I am, still surprised by life. How to describe it? It's a peculiar feeling, one I've never had before. It's like I'm somehow connected to people. I've always been a bit of a loner, always let Rose handle the people thing, so it's strange for me. Well, so be it. Rose always said those were my words for everything.

*

I'm not sure when it started – hold on, yes, I do know. It was this Monday. I remember because I ventured outside. The weather was fine, so I took my shoes in to be resoled. Down there on the corner.

I was walking along and paused to catch my breath, just took a minute to steady myself there by the churchyard railing. Along came a young mother with a baby carriage. She stopped to adjust the soft blue blanket around a tiny baby. I nodded politely, and glanced down at her baby. He looked like he was born that day, a brand-new little thing.

And that's when it happened. He opened his eyes and looked at me. For the briefest of moments, our eyes met, and I *knew* I had seen that baby before, a long time ago. And I knew that he recognized me, too.

I looked up in astonishment at his mother, but she just smiled and continued down the sidewalk. I stood there a moment and watched them leave. Then I scratched my head and thought it must be my age playing tricks on me.

The shoe man said he'd have my shoes ready the next day. I have to say, he's one of the best cobblers I've ever had the pleasure to come across in this long life of mine. His name is Ignatius, but in my mind I call him Giuseppe. He looks like the old mustached fella in that fairytale. I told him if the weather holds I'd be in the next day to pick them up.

Giuseppe? No, hold on, that's not it. Geppetto – that's it. I couldn't help but chuckle when I watched him through the window, bending over his table of shoes. I wondered if he had a little wooden puppet in the back room there.

*

Well, the weather did hold so I went and got my shoes. I can't swear to it, but I think I saw a few buds on the churchyard trees. It seems a little early, but then again, I've seen spring arrive as early as February and as late as May. Spring can be unpredictable, and it's best to respect her fickle ways. Never plant tomatoes before May tenth. That's just a fact of life round here.

One year, I just couldn't wait, and I planted them on the ninth. Rose told me not to. She said it had taken so long to raise the tomatoes from seeds to seedlings, why not wait another day?

But I was a stubborn young cur back then, before Rose's gentle ways had a chance to work on me. And dang, if it didn't freeze that night! Lost the whole lot of them. She never said a word then, but we laughed about it for years.

Anyway, there I was, resting on the church-yard bench, with my resoled shoes in a bag and my cane propped alongside me. From the side door of the church, came a small group of people. A proud father carried a baby dressed in a long, white christening gown.

I stood as they walked by me and tipped my hat. They reminded me of Rose and me and our firstborn. People tipped their hats back then. I guess I looked a little odd, but they just smiled. The beaming mother positioned the child, so I could see it.

"What a beautiful baby," I said.

And dang if it didn't happen again! The baby locked eyes with me and smiled a knowing smile, smiled in recognition!

I looked up at the parents, astonished once again. But they thought I was astonished by the charm of their baby, said, "Thank you," and left.

I faltered to the bench, and for some reason clutched the shoe bag and cane for all I was worth.

What was going on here? Something new was happening. Ole Life was at his tricks again.

But I have to say, this was a welcome trick. It's rather nice to be recognized after so many years of outliving everyone.

*

I wish I could tell Rose about this new thing. She would be able to make sense of it. She would come up with some explanation.

My Rose. When I first saw her, my heart stopped. She had moved into the house down the street. I'd been back from the war for about a year and was studying on the GI Bill. I was heading to the trolley on my way to the school library, books in arm. And there she was, coming down the front porch steps in some kind of hurry, adjusting her little hat, and nearly ran smack into me. She didn't, but I dropped my books all the same. She stood there and laughed – our eyes locked and we laughed. We both knew that I had dropped my books from the effect of her beauty on me.

Well, I was smitten, as they say. She helped me pick up my books. Normally, I would not have allowed a woman to do such a thing, but that time I did – because it gave me a few more moments to look at her.

One thing led to another. We courted, and wed within the year. We were married on a

Wednesday, but it was a Saturday when I first saw her and fell in love.

I had this little game I played: I used to buy her roses on the anniversary of the day I first saw her. Roses for my Rose. She didn't know what a momentous day it had been for me. Oh, sure, I brought her flowers throughout the year. She always loved them so. Rose was raised in the country and was used to blooming things, and she missed that when her family moved to the city. So I bought her flowers, whatever I could find in season.

But on the seventeenth of every May, I came home with a bunch of roses, different colors. She especially liked those orangey pink ones, but I couldn't always find them.

"What's the occasion?" she'd ask.

And I'd say, "Oh, nothing special."

But after a couple of years, she finally caught on. She cried when she figured it out. My soft-hearted Rose.

*

I didn't feel so good today. I think it's my heart. It jumps and starts and then slows of its own accord. Maybe it was all that thinking about Rose. A tightening in my chest, like on the day I first saw her.

My granddaughter drove me to the hospital – made me go. I didn't want to come here. I'd rather be home. She stops by every Thursday. Sometimes we go to lunch or to the park. She's been pestering me to come live with her, but I like my apartment. I'm comfortable there. If I moved to the suburb I would miss my neighborhood, the church being so close, the corner grocery, the diner, and people like Giuseppe.

When they wheeled me into the hospital, I thought people were looking at me funny, like they were expecting me or something. All so friendly. Or maybe I was looking funny at them. Now this thing is happening, I catch myself studying everyone closely, to see if I recognize them or not.

*

Can't say I like being here. Hospitals are strange places. Too many bells and whistles going off at all hours. But I have the kindest people tending to me. Again, I had the sensation that I knew them. The nurse looked so familiar to me as she read my chart.

Then a young Negro fella came in – an orderly, I think they call them. I looked at him, and when he smiled at me I had that same feeling, like I knew him well. He had an accent of some kind. I stared at him and asked if we had met before somewhere. He laughed, and said not unless I had been to Cameroon. But when I looked at him I knew, just *knew*, that we had been best buddies a long, long time ago.

I'm afraid I stared at him rather intently, trying to place him, but he didn't seem to mind. He was so gentle and considerate. He checked on me throughout the night, and patted my shoulder when he thought I was asleep.

When his shift was over, he introduced me to his replacement. I thought he said her name was Rose, but I must have mixed things up. Then he took my hand, and said something I couldn't make out. I wanted to reply, but I couldn't talk with all that paraphernalia in me. But he nodded and smiled, just as if he'd heard me.

*

Been thinking of Rose nonstop. It's like she's here with me. And today's a Saturday, well what do you know! I couldn't open my eyes, but I knew she was right here with me. I felt her hand on mine all through the night, felt the lightest kiss on my cheek now and then, just the way she used to do. I've never felt her so close as I do now.

*

That wily fellow Life just had to give me one final tap on the shoulder and show me one last thing. For I know that's me laid out in the casket there. Yet here I am, standing and looking on at my own funeral. In my Sunday best, with my Rose beside me looking radiant and holding my hand tightly, like this time she's not going to let go.

I guess I should be sad, and I do feel a certain pity for my old frail self lying there. And I wish I could comfort my grieving granddaughter.

But I have to say that I've never been happier. Rose is tugging at my sleeve now, smiling, and saying, "Come on – let's go see the children."

If that isn't the dangdest thing.